ALFIE

Alfie at Nursery School

Shirley Hughes

Red Fox

The Treehouse

Every weekday morning Alfie went to Parkside Nursery School. His best friend Bernard went there too, and so did Min and Neal and Sam and lots of his other friends.

There were plenty of interesting things to do there.

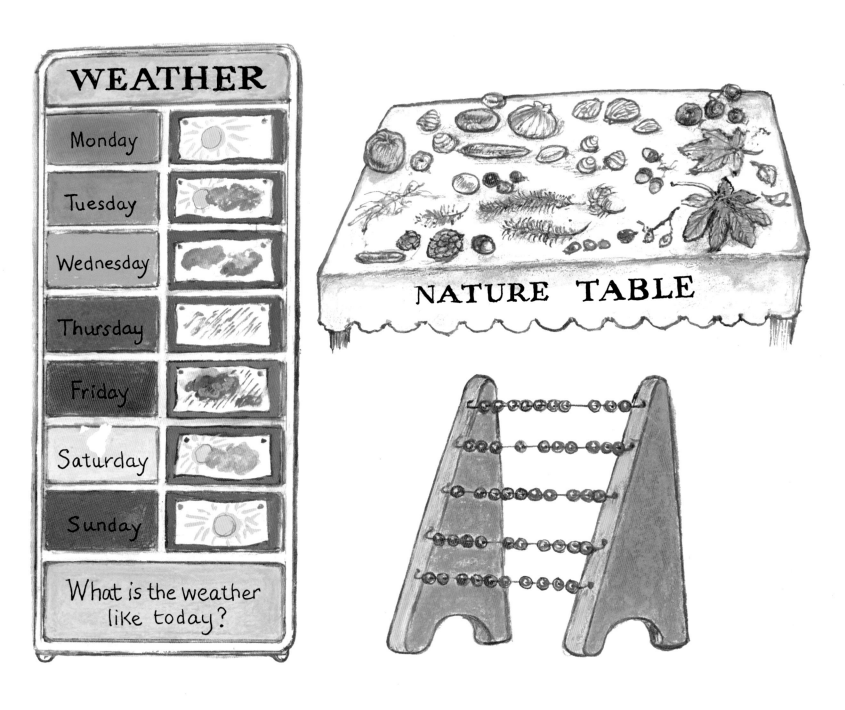

WEATHER

Monday	
Tuesday	
Wednesday	
Thursday	
Friday	
Saturday	
Sunday	

What is the weather like today?

NATURE TABLE

They did counting

and drew pictures

and did lots of writing practice.

They drew around their hands and coloured them in.

And at Easter they painted and decorated a big egg.

At playtime they went outside into a big leafy yard
where they could do skipping and play with hoops
and pour out water into measuring jugs.

They played "catch" with beanbags

and ran in and out of cones.

There was a big sandpit and a climbing frame and a lovely little tree house.

One day two boys called Walter and Ben told everyone that they were going to start a club in the tree house, and only their special friends like Raymond and Harry were going to be asked to join.

They had made stick-on badges for all the members.
They said that no girls were going to be allowed in
except Mandy Drew and Rosa Bathgate.

When they all had their badges, they solemnly filed up the steps to the tree
house, leaving a notice at the bottom saying: "PRIVAT-CLUB MEMBERS ONLY".

Bernard did not mind a bit about not being
asked to join Walter and Ben's club.
"Come on, Alfie," he said.
"Let's go and play in the sandpit!"

All through playtime Walter and Ben and the other club members stayed in the tree house. They stayed there and stayed there for quite a long time.

Mandy was the first to leave. She slipped away to join some other friends who were having a skipping game.

Then two of the other boy
members got bored
and drifted away.

Rosa stayed for quite a long
time. But in the end Walter
and Ben were the only members
left there. They looked out at
Alfie and Bernard and all
the other children playing
in the yard.

"Want to play a game of catch with Alfie and me?" Bernard called up to them.

"Sure," answered Walter as he and Ben climbed down to join them.

At the next playtime there were plenty of people in the tree house, but Walter and Ben gave it a miss for the time being. They had disbanded their club. They had both decided it was more fun if anyone who wanted to could go in the tree house, even if they didn't have a special badge.

The Concert

Alfie's little sister Annie Rose very much wanted to go to Parkside Nursery School with Alfie, but she was too little.

Every morning when she and Mum said goodbye to Alfie at the gate she tried to get out of her buggy to go with him. "You'll be able to come here one day," Alfie told her kindly. "But you are not big enough yet."

This did not cheer Annie Rose up.
She wanted to go there now.
She kicked her feet about crossly when
she saw him go in with his friends.

Soon there was going to be a special day at the nursery school
when all the families were invited to come to a midsummer concert.
The children had done a lot of rehearsing for it.

Some were going to play drums and triangles
and tambourines, and some were going to sing.
Bernard was going to play a drum, and Alfie was a singer.

When the day of the concert came,
all the tables were cleared away
and there were flowers everywhere.

As all the mums and dads and grandmas and grandpas and older sisters and brothers arrived, they were each given one of the lovely programmes which the children had painted.

When everyone was seated, Mr Hunter, one of their nursery school teachers, struck up a tune on the piano, and all the children began to sing and play their very best.

But then a very embarrassing thing happened . . .

Annie Rose wriggled off Mum's lap and ran up in front
of all the audience to stand next to Alfie.

She was determined to join in with the singing,
though of course she did not know the words.

Alfie went pink in the face.
He looked across at Mum.
And Mum looked at him.

They both knew very well that
if either of them tried to make
Annie Rose go back to her seat
she would make a terrible fuss.

So Alfie took her hand tightly and went on singing. Luckily Annie Rose behaved very well.

She just stood there, proudly beaming at everyone.

And when that part of the concert was over and they all clapped, she ran back to sit on Mum's lap again, as good as gold.

"Having a little sister is a lot of RESPONSIBILITY sometimes,"
Alfie said to Mum when they were getting ready to go home.

"That's a very long word," said Mum. "And you're quite right. But you
saved the concert for everyone, Alfie, and I'm ever so proud of you!"